A King Production presents…

*A Titillating*
*Tale*

*A Novelette*

# JOY DEJA KING

ISBN 13: 978-1958834015
ISBN 10: 1-958834-01-7
Cover concept by Joy Deja King
Library of Congress Cataloging-in-Publication Data;
A King Production
Deadly Divorce...A Titillating Tale by Joy Deja King
Graphic design: www.anitaart79.wixsite.com/bookdesign
Typesetting: Anita J.

For complete Library of Congress Copyright info visit;
www.joydejaking.com
Twitter @joydejaking

A King Production
P.O. Box 912, Collierville, TN 38027
A King Production and the above portrayal log are trademarks
of A King Production LLC

This Novelette is Dedicated To My:

Family, Readers, and Supporters.
I LOVE you guys so much. Please believe that!!

—Joy Deja King

A special THANK YOU to RG, for motivating me
to get back to doing what I love. I will always
adore you. For Life.

—Joy Deja King

"Can't Be No Nigga Ex
I Could Only Be His Widow
That's A Fact Dressed In Black
My Heart Break, Bones Will Crack ..."

~Cardi B ~

A KING PRODUCTION

# Deadly Divorce...

*A Titillating Tale*

TOXIC SERIES

*A Novelette*

# JOY DEJA KING

# Chapter One

# Banking On Me

"What do you mean I didn't get the part?" Londyn swallowed hard. "You said the casting director loved me."

"Chris does," her agent Misty confirmed.

"Then what happened?!" Londyn's tone was loud and hostile, causing people in the restaurant to turnaround and briefly stare. She took a deep breath and lowered her voice. "When I got the callback and auditioned for the casting director and director, they both seemed extremely pleased with my audition. You even said I was a shoo-in for the role, so what happened?"

"You know I'm always transparent with you," Misty sighed. "Well, as you're aware the production is a big budget film and is supposed to be on track for box office gold."

"Exactly! This role was finally going to get me off the B-list and make me an A-list superstar."

"And you know I want that for you. You deserve it, and I still believe it will happen," she added.

"Stop bullshitting me and tell me why I didn't get the part," Londyn fumed.

"Supposedly, they're saying the producer requested a specific actress to be attached to the production who has the ability to fill up the movie theater. But off the record, Chris confided in me that the producer went over his head and the director, pulled some strings, and got the actress he wanted," Misty explained.

"Who is she?"

Misty hesitated for a moment. "Veronica Woods...I know I know," she put her hands up and said, knowing what Londyn was going to say next.

"Veronica! She can't fill up an elementary school play let alone a movie theater," Londyn seethed. "She's barely C-list!"

"Listen, everything you're saying, I said it and more with expletives. I'm being calm now, but I was livid. Chris finally admitted to me that whoever Veronica is dating, the producer owes him a huge favor and he called it in."

"So, Veronica got the part that I busted my ass off for, because of who she's fuckin'." Londyn rolled her eyes looking completely defeated.

"We both know this industry can be cruel and there's nothing fair about it. I hate seeing this disappointment on your face, but we'll push through like we always do," Misty said placing her hand on Londyn's arm.

"I just knew it was finally my time," Londyn's voice trailed off, she said shaking her head.

"Chris really is a fan of yours. He thought you were perfect for the lead but because of the Veronica situation, he offered you another part. Of course, it's a much smaller role but it will give you an opportunity to be seen by millions of people."

"I don't think I'm interested in his consolation prize."

"Londyn, don't look at it that way. View it as an opportunity to shine. This could lead to a bigger role in another movie."

"How many times have I heard that." Londyn's attitude had become cynical. "I'm not eighteen, just getting off the bus. I've been doing this for over ten years, and I feel like I've been stuck. My career seems to have reached a plateau. I'll never be a bankable actress."

"That's not necessarily true. Lots of talented and beautiful actresses don't reach superstar status until much later in their career," Misty said with optimism in her voice. From the dismal expression on Londyn's face, she could see her words of encouragement weren't working. "Just consider taking the other role Chris is offering you. And don't forget, ABC really wants you for their new crime drama."

"I'm not interested in doing a television show, plus the networks are saturated with crime dramas. The show will probably be cancelled after the first season," Londyn complained.

"Will you at least consider the smaller role Chris is offering...please," Misty pleaded.

"Sure, I'll think about it," Londyn exhaled, standing up. "But I have to go. I don't want to be late for Ryan's first major exhibit at that art gallery tonight, so I need to get to my hair appointment," she said grabbing her purse.

"That's right, Ryan's exhibit is tonight. Let him know I never received my invite."

"I told you he said that was an oversight and you are most definitely invited. He'll be disappointed if you don't show up."

"I highly doubt that, but if you insist, I guess I can come," Misty smirked. "Besides, I heard it's the place to be tonight. Ryan must be elated."

"More like thankful he is finally getting the recognition he deserves. Ryan has always had a vision and stayed focused. It's going to be amazing to see his vision come to life." Londyn smiled proudly at how far her friend had come, and the direction his career was heading in.

"A minute ago I was worried the frown on your face was permanent but now that winning smile is back. I'll have to thank Ryan when I see him tonight."

"Yeah, I'll have to thank him too. He inspires me. We both got to LA around the same time. After all the time and work he's put in at the studio, Ryan has finally gotten his big breakthrough. Maybe that means my big break is coming too," Londyn winked.

Misty desperately wanted the same thing for Londyn. She still remembered the day Londyn walked into her office begging for representation. She read a feature Variety Magazine had recently done on Misty and was adamant she was the only agent for her. She was so full of passion yet extremely stubborn, refusing to take no for an answer. That was the main reason Misty couldn't deny her request, although she was a complete unknown. Londyn soon became her favorite client. She had this sparkle and tenacity in her eyes that made you root for her. She still had that same spark, but Misty was afraid that if Londyn didn't reach the success she desired, that fire would soon burn out.

# Chapter Two

## *He Had Me At Hello*

"Ryan, this is unbelievable. I'm so, so proud of you!" Londyn gushed giving one of her closest friends a hug. "If I have my way, every piece of your artwork is going to sell tonight."

"Thank you for saying that and for being here. This seems a bit unreal to me. I keep praying it ain't all a dream," Ryan confessed.

"It's real and no one is more deserving," Londyn assured him. "And I must say, the growth with your artwork is amazing. I love every painting."

"Speaking of amazing, look at you. How is it you get more beautiful every time I see you."

"Stop it. Tonight, is all about you. You can rave about my beauty any ole day," Londyn cackled, playfully hitting Ryan's shoulder. "But real talk, instead of being over here with me, I think you have a potential buyer over there," Londyn said nodding her head towards the owner of the gallery who was trying to get Ryan's attention.

"I'll be back beautiful," he said giving Londyn a kiss on the cheek. After Ryan walked away, Londyn continued admiring the abstract art adorning the wall. The tasteful blend of colors and shapes, which resembled reality but masterfully failed, was emotionally impactful to her.

"The artwork is almost as intriguing as you."

"Excuse me?" Londyn turned to see who was speaking to her. She was met with a man who had penetrating eyes, an irresistible face and a statuesque athletic built body.

"Hello. I'm Sterling and you are Londyn Lewis. It's a pleasure to meet you," he said extending his well-manicured hand.

"Hi." Londyn shook his hand. "For some reason I feel like we've met before."

"No, I would've remembered. I've been a fan of yours since I saw you in Love and Lies."

"Oh gosh. You would mention the movie I spent the majority of time in barely there lingerie," Londyn said putting her head down in shame.

"You should be proud and holding your head up high. You were incredible in that movie. Wait till I tell my best friend Kash that I met Sage from the movie Love and Lies."

"Please stop. I hardly had any lines in that movie," she remarked.

"Trust me, your role was memorable," Sterling countered. "But enough about Love and Lies, I want to get to know you, not the character Sage you played."

"Really?" Londyn found herself blushing which was unexpected. "What do you want to know about me?"

"Everything. I'm surrounded by so much, but I'm most intrigued by you. That's saying a lot since we're at an exhibit with some extraordinary artwork."

"You're really embarrassing me," Londyn admitted, feeling like an awkward teenager with a schoolgirl crush.

"That's not my intention. I just want to get to know you," he said taking her hand.

Sterling's touch triggered strong hidden emotions within Londyn. There was this feeling of sexual arousal that was startling, and she wanted it to stop but it seemed out of her control.

"I really should go. This is my friend's exhibit, and I promised to help him sell every piece of artwork tonight. Standing here, staring into your eyes is not going to make that happen. I need to do some mingling," Londyn said not wanting to let go.

"Come have a drink with me. There's a place right across the street. We can have some privacy. I promise not to keep you long."

"I can't leave. I have to stay and support my friend."

'Then have dinner with me tomorrow and I refuse to take no for an answer. Don't make me beg, but I will," Sterling persisted.

"Yes, I'll have dinner with you tomorrow."

Sterling stood close to Londyn, sweeping her hair behind her ear. "Tomorrow will be the most unbelievable night of your life," he whispered, sending a chill down her spine.

Londyn woke up fixated on one thing, her dinner date with Sterling tonight. She fell asleep dreaming about him, it was now morning, and nothing had changed. She stretched her arms in bed, welcoming the warmth of the sun coming through her bedroom window. This was the first time since Londyn arrived in LA to pursue an acting career that she woke up with something on her mind other than work, and she welcomed the change. As she glided around her high-rise apartment daydreaming about Sterling, she almost missed the call from Misty.

"Good morning!" Londyn answered cheerfully.

"I see you woke up on the right side of the bed. I can't remember the last time I heard your voice sound so extra chipper," Misty commented.

"What can I say, I have a lot to be excited about."

"Yes, you do. I'm glad you've come around to seeing things my way." Misty stated confidently. "I knew if you thought about it, you'd realize that taking this role is the right move for your career. Chris will be pleased when I deliver the news."

"My upbeat voice has nothing to do with that movie. Now that I think about it, the movie nor that role has crossed my mind."

"Wait...what?" Misty took Londyn off speaker and put the phone close to her ear, as if that was going to make her hear something different.

"My excitement has nothing to do with work. I met someone. A man who I can't stop thinking about."

Misty could see Londyn's smile through the phone, she was gushing so hard. "Out of all the years I've known you, besides your father, who went on to a better place many years ago, the only man who has put a smile on your face is Ryan, who you have a platonic relationship with. So, who is this man that has you all giddy?"

"His name is Sterling. I met him last night at Ryan's art exhibit. He touched my hand and I literally wanted to melt. I've never felt this way before."

"Girl please!" Misty scoffed. "That feeling you got comes from a lack of sex. I told you a few months ago you needed to get fucked really good. But you dismissed my advice. Now the first man that touches your hand, you think something magical is happening."

"Yeah, it's been a while, but I've had sex before and I've been touched by enough men to know this was different. It wasn't just his touch; it was also the way he looked at me, even his voice made me weak."

"Oh damn, don't make me throw up in my

mouth. Can you please put my client back on the phone instead of this imposter pretending to be Londyn Lewis," Misty mocked.

"You're being absurd. I thought you would be happy for me but obviously, I was wrong. It doesn't matter though because tonight I'm having dinner with a man who has awaken all these emotions inside of me that I didn't even know existed. And I plan on embracing every second of it."

"Londyn, I need you to stay focused on the prize and it's not a man. Remember that blockbuster film you want to headline and that Oscar..."

"Misty, I have to hit you back. That's Ryan calling me," Londyn said ending their call. "Hey you!" She answered, not allowing her agent and friend to ruin her blissful mood."

"Good morning to you. I wanted to catch you before you headed out for your morning workout."

"I'm running a little behind, so you caught me at the perfect time. Did you wake up still relishing in that mind-blowing exhibit you had last night? And whoever did your PR deserves a huge bonus. I mean there was the perfect mixture of artists, athletes, actors and corporate bigwigs there."

"Richard, the gallery owner hired the PR company, and they did deliver the goods and so did you. Did you win the lottery and forget to tell yo' boy?" Ryan questioned.

"Huh, what goods did I deliver?" Londyn was completely thrown off by Ryan's comment.

"You bought all the paintings I had for sale. I was speechless when I got the call this morning. Richard lost his shit because you know his commission will be ridiculous. Londyn, I can't believe you did that for me."

"I didn't! I don't have coins like that," she gasped. "I wish I could afford to buy all your artwork because that would mean I was a rich bitch. We both know that ain't true."

"That's why I asked if you hit the lotto or some shit."

"Maybe you misunderstood what Richard said."

"Nope, I didn't misunderstand him. You attached a note with the cashier's check," Ryan informed her.

"What did the note say?" she was downright baffled.

"Something along the lines of, making good on a promise to help me sell every piece of artwork and the note was signed Love Londyn."

"WTF!!" she exclaimed. Then there was a short pause as her mind began to spin. "Oh my fuckin' goodness." Londyn sat down on the sofa in disbelief. "Sterling must've left that cashier's check and note."

"What are you talkin' about...and who is Sterling?"

"This man I met last night at your exhibit. We were talking and I mentioned that I needed to go mingle because I promised you, I would make sure you sold all your artwork."

"And you think he was the one that cut the check? That sounds a bit farfetched." Ryan wasn't convinced.

"I didn't cut the check, nor write the note. Sterling was the only person I shared that comment with besides you. It has to be him."

"If you're right, that must've been some talk you all had," he cracked.

"I guess I'll have to ask him tonight over dinner."

"You're having dinner with him tonight, like a date?" Ryan sounded surprised.

"Yes. Why do you sound shocked? That's what people do, go out on dates."

"Most people but not you. The only time I remember you going on a date is when you lost that bet. Your attitude was you had plenty of time to find a man after you achieved the career you wanted," Ryan reminded his friend.

"Maybe my attitude needs some adjustments. We can finish discussing this later. I have a lot to get done before my date with Sterling tonight. We'll chat later. Love you, Ryan!" Londyn blew him a kiss and hung up before he could say another word.

# Chapter Three

*Man Of My Dreams*

"Did I tell you how beautiful you look tonight," Sterling said admiring how sexy yet subtle the rose and leopard printed low back silk swing dress with gold chain straps accentuated her body.

"Yes, you did tell me a few times, but I love hearing it," Londyn smiled.

"I love telling you, although I'm sure you're used to men complimenting your beauty all the time over dinner."

"Not really. This is the first date I've been on in eons."

"Stop lying," Sterling laughed placing his wine glass on the table.

"I'm serious. Since the day I arrived in LA, I've been laser focused on my acting career. Going out on dates was not a priority for me."

"Does that mean I'm not just another one of your admirers you decided to have dinner with, and I should feel lucky?"

"I don't think lucky is the right word choice. But what about me? There are a ton of beautiful women in LA. Should I feel like I'm just one of many you have private candlelight romantic dinners with?" Londyn asked.

"You are certainly not one of many, you are the one," Sterling leaned forward and said.

"You have this way of making me blush," she admitted modestly, shifting her gaze and glancing down.

"Why is that?" Sterling moved Londyn's hair back and lifted her chin so he could stare directly in her eyes.

"I guess because I'm so drawn to you, and I'm not used to feeling that way. But I like it because you also make me feel special."

"You are special and if you let me, I'll show you every single day for the rest of your life."

"The way you said that I almost believe you."

Londyn continued to blush, feeling self-conscious with how physically attracted and sexually excited Sterling made her.

"You should believe me because it's true."

"Can I ask you a question? I think I know the answer, but I still have to ask."

"Of course," he said leaning back in his chair.

"Were you the one who bought all of Ryan's paintings?"

"Well, technically it came from you, I just provided the funds."

"I can't believe you did something so generous."

"You think that's generous?"

"Is that a serious question or are you joking?" Londyn raised an eyebrow. "Because I've never had a man do something like that on my behalf before."

"You just hadn't met the right man, but you have now." Sterling's bold confidence made his appeal even more intoxicating to Londyn. She wanted to be with him in every way, to the point she had to stop herself from hoping on top of his dick and riding him right there underneath the moonlit sky. The only reason she held back was because she didn't want to come across as sex deprived and desperate.

"How do you know you're the right man for me?"

"Because you're the perfect woman for me, so I must be the right man for you."

"Wow, if what you're saying is true, then I guess there's no need for me to ever go on another date again. I should date you exclusively," Londyn teased.

"Would you like some more wine before we leave?"

"After devouring the chocolate expresso cake, I'm completely stuffed. But thank you for an amazing evening, I've never had dinner on the rooftop of a high rise building with a breathtaking skyline view. And there's no one here but the two of us," Londyn enthused, resting the side of her face on her hands. "How romantic is that."

"The evening isn't over yet. There's more to come," Sterling said taking Londyn's hand. "A helicopter will be landing here shortly to take us to our next destination."

"Are you serious?" Londyn's eyes widened with anticipation. "Where are we going...wait don't tell me, I want it to be a surprise." She was swept up in the moment, falling into Sterling's arms.

"Good afternoon gorgeous," Sterling said kissing Londyn on the forehead.

"What time is it?" she asked sitting up in the bed.

"Two o'clock. Are you hungry?"

"Starving," Londyn said rubbing her eyes. "Did you cook this for me?" she questioned taking the tray of food from him.

"No, I can't take credit, I ordered you some room service."

"That's right, we did spend the night at a hotel. You know I had the craziest dream that we took a helicopter to Vegas and got married." After the words left Londyn's mouth, she glanced down at her hand and saw a wedding ring on her finger.

"It wasn't a dream. You're Mrs. Sterling Pierce," he said sitting down on the bed next to Londyn. Are you okay with that?"

"Of course I'm okay with that! I remember everything from last night so vividly, but it seemed too perfect to be true. I was convinced it was a dream to spare myself from disappointment. I thought maybe I had too much champagne and it was all in my head."

"It's not in your head. Everything you remember, actually happened," he assured her.

So, I'm your wife!" Londyn couldn't contain her excitement.

"Yes, you're my wife."

"This is the happiest day of my life!" She hugged Sterling tightly.

"Mine too," he said kissing his new bride. "And so, you know, that ring is temporary. We can go to the jewelry store, and you can pick out whatever you like or have a wedding ring custom designed. It's up to you."

"How did I get so lucky. You're like the man of my dreams."

"I'm the lucky one," he said kissing Londyn once again before standing up. "I need to make a few business calls, so I'll leave you to eat your food. I love you."

"I love you too," Londyn smiled, blowing kisses to her husband as he walked out the room. She was basking in the moment when she heard her phone vibrating on the nightstand. "Hello Misty!"

"Hello to you. I thought you were going to call me this morning."

"My apologies. I just woke up."'

"You do realize it's the middle of the afternoon."

"Yes, but I had a super long night."

"I see." She stated curtly. "Well, I just got off the phone with Chris. He's still waiting for your decision. I was tempted to tell him yes you would take the role, but I wanted to confirm with you first," Misty said sounding impatient.

"About that role. I think I'm going to pass."

"Excuse me?" Misty went from sounding impatient to angry.

"I'm a newlywed. I got married last night," Londyn announced with delight. "I think I should spend some quality time with my husband instead of hopping on a plane to film a movie that I'm not even the star of."

"You better be fuckin' kidding me," Misty barked.

"No congratulations?"

"Congratulate you for what! I don't even know who the fuck your husband is. Please tell me you're joking, Londyn. Surely, I haven't been your agent and friend for all these years just to be blindsided by you with some bogus marriage," Misty scolded.

"Tell me how you really feel," Londyn hissed.

"I just did," Misty snapped back.

"It's not a joke. Sterling and I got married last

night in Vegas. I'm now Mrs., Sterling Pierce," she stated proudly, staring at her wedding ring.

"Wait—you don't mean Sterling Pierce who's a partner in that Venture Capital Firm?"

"Honestly, I never asked him what he did for a living," Londyn giggled like a lovesick schoolgirl. "But he has to be successful based on this whirlwind romance we've been on."

"If you're married to *the* Sterling Pierce, successful is an understatement. He is filthy fuckin' rich."

"Really...rich like that?" Londyn was a bit astounded by the news. She figured he was well off but by the way Misty was talking, it was next level type rich shit.

"Check the text message I just sent you," Misty said.

"That picture doesn't do Sterling justice but that's my husband," she confirmed.

"Did you sign a prenup?"

"No. It all happened so fast and without any advance preparation. But I wouldn't have a problem signing a postnuptial agreement. I know we live in LA, and this probably sounds cliché, but I married Sterling for love not money."

"When you mentioned meeting a man named Sterling at Ryan's art exhibit, never did I think you were speaking of Sterling Pierce. Now you're his wife. Only in Hollywood!" Misty exclaimed, shaking her head.

"Hollywood wife Londyn Pierce...I like the sound of that." She stated. "Maybe it's time for me to put my acting career on hold for a minute or two," Londyn reasoned.

"As your agent and friend, I advise you to slow down. Don't make anymore life changing decisions until you settle into your marriage."

"Fine, but I have to go. My food is getting cold. I'll call you when I get back to LA.," Londyn said ending the call abruptly. She wasn't in the mood to hear disparaging commentary from Misty, friend or not.

Londyn was aware she didn't have a conventional courtship with Sterling, but it didn't make their marriage any less authentic. They were now husband and wife. Misty and anyone else who had a problem with their union would have to deal with it or stay out of her life.

# Chapter Four

## Mr. & Mrs. Sterling Pierce

"Thank you all for coming this evening," Sterling said with Londyn standing by his side on the terrace overlooking the lush, landscaped garden at their chateau-esque private mansion. "For most of you, this is your first time meeting my beautiful wife Londyn," he said kissing her hand. "I knew she was the one, the moment I laid eyes on her which is why several weeks ago, I didn't hesitate to fly off to Vegas to get married. She is the only woman for me," he continued gazing into her eyes. "We will be together for life, so I appreciate each of you being here to celebrate this momentous occasion with us."

The large crowd erupted in applause, with many holding up their champagne glasses sending well wishes to the newlywed couple. You could feel their love in the air which made the guests cheer for a happily ever after.

"I didn't think you were coming but I'm thrilled you're here," Londyn said embracing Misty with an endearing hug.

"Since I couldn't make it to the wedding, I felt compelled to come to the afterparty," Misty joked. "But seriously, I might not agree with every decision you make but I will always be here to show my support because I love you."

"I know you do, and I love you too." The women embraced for another hug.

"I have to admit, being the wife of a filthy rich man sure does look fuckin' fabulous on you," Misty winked glancing around the opulent estate. "A mega mansion in exclusive Holmby Hills. That massive rock on your finger," she said holding up Londyn's left hand to get a closer look at the custom-made emerald cut ring designed by Jean Dousset which was surrounded by a halo of diamonds and set on a double diamond pave band.

"Does that mean you're no longer upset with me for declining that movie role?"

"No, I'm not mad but a script did come across my desk the other day. And I believe you're perfect for the leading role. The director called me personally wanting you to audition."

"I can't."

"Can't you at least read the script first? You might fall in love with the character. Just read it," Misty pressed.

"It wouldn't matter if it was the most incredible part I ever read, I still couldn't do it," Londyn said.

"Why not?"

"I'm pregnant," she revealed in a low voice. "You're the first person I told besides my mother, sister and of course my husband, so please don't tell anyone. I want to get past the first trimester before making any announcements."

"You're going to make me cry," Misty said getting choked up. "Can we hug one more time?"

"Yes!" Both women laughed.

"You know I'm not the sentimental type, and for a long time I didn't think you were either," Misty cracked. "But first the wedding and now the baby news, this is really tugging at my heart. I never knew you even wanted kids."

"I didn't, or so I thought. But everything changed when I met Sterling," Londyn professed glancing over at her husband who was surrounded by a bevy of beautiful women, his best friend and business partner Kash, and a few other men, who were hanging on to his every word. None of that surprised her as he had that effect on people. Sterling was handsome but more than that he was charismatic. He would draw you so far in that you prayed he would never let you go.

"The two of you really do make a beautiful couple. I'm truly happy for you Londyn. You deserve a happy ending," Misty said kissing her on the cheek. "I would love to stay longer and do some socializing, but I have an overseas zoom call early in the morning. I want to go home and try to get a few hours of sleep."

"I totally understand, I'm just glad you came." While Londyn was giving Misty one last hug before she left, she noticed Ryan and her sister walking in their direction. "Can you stay one minute longer?" she asked. "I want you to take a pic with Ryan and my sister."

"Of course!" Misty happily agreed. "Hey Ryan, and Jayla it's so good to see you again! It's been too long," Misty beamed wrapping her arms around Londyn's sister.

"It's good to see you also! But we should be seeing a lot more of each other since I'm staying in LA permanently."

"Really...you're moving here? I had no idea," Misty said.

"Neither did I," Londyn chimed in. "When did you make this decision?"

"I'd been considering it but after discussing the idea with Ryan, I think it's the right decision," Jayla smiled widely.

"I think that's a fantastic idea!" Londyn clapped her hands together. "I'll have my little sister here with me."

"Does that mean I can live here with you and Sterling?" Jayla asked.

"Yes! Why would you even ask such a silly question. Besides, it can get lonely in that big ass house, especially since Sterling is always working. So, I welcome your company."

"Awesome! You're the best, Londyn!"

"Stop it! Now come over here, so we can take this group picture," Londyn said pulling Misty and Ryan next to them, before calling over the photographer. She wanted to capture this moment in time as everything in her life seemed perfectly aligned...almost too perfect.

# Chapter Five

## *Everlasting Love*

*One Year Later...*

"My beautiful son," Sterling said cradling Easton in his arms. "Each day I hold him he gets bigger and more handsome."

"Yes, he does. He gets his good looks from his father," Londyn said standing behind her husband, wrapping her arms around his waist.

"His mother isn't lacking in the looks department either," Sterling said, turning to kiss his wife. "What do you and Easton have planned for the day?"

"I have a few interviews with some potential nannies and then we're having a late lunch with Misty."

"Are you sure you even want a nanny?"

"Yes, why would you ask me that?"

"Because you've been interviewing nannies since before Easton was even born, and you find some reason not to hire them. Many of whom have been highly qualified."

"I just want to make sure I hire the right person. They are going to be helping with our precious baby," Londyn said placing Easton in her arms.

"I'm all for being cautious but everyone that comes in for an interview has been well vetted. Our son will be fine. Plus, I want some alone time with my gorgeous wife, so we can go on dates again or even get away for the weekend."

"Jayla doesn't mind babysitting if I need her to."

"Your sister is young and should be able to hang out with her own friends, not be the designated babysitter."

"You're right, I guess I'm not ready to have this little one out of my sight," she placed Easton's soft head against her cheek, inhaling his clean, yet sweet smell. "I never knew someone could love and need me so much," she said gazing in her son's eyes.

"Your husband loves and needs you too."

"You're absolutely right, my love." Londyn gave Sterling a long, passionate kiss.

"Now that was nice. More kisses like that and we'll end up making another baby," he remarked.

"I like the idea of making baby number two," Londyn beamed.

"Babe, I was joking. Let's enjoy Easton for a few years, then we can consider having another baby. Besides, you finally got your figure back. No need to gamble again so soon and take another chance messing with perfection," he said kissing Londyn goodbye. "I need to get to the office. I'll see you later on tonight."

Londyn let out a deep sigh, choosing to disregard what her husband said. She walked over to the walls of glass opening to a massive wraparound terrace off the master suite, admiring the picturesque lake and garden with stone fountains and sweeping views of the surrounding mountains.

"One day soon I'll be sitting out here watching you run around playing." Londyn was speaking out loud what she visualized her son's future to be, while cradling him in her arms. "Wouldn't it be perfect if you had a little sister running around playing with you too," she said staring directly at Easton as if she expected him to respond.

The life Londyn had been living for over a year as a wife and now a mother, was never the one she had dreamed of. But it had quickly become the only life she could imagine living. Easton filled her heart with such unconditional love and had become her greatest gift. She had her husband to thank for that, so she wanted to do everything within her power to also make him happy.

"Easton, mommy is going to find you the perfect nanny, so I can start spending some quality time with your daddy. I'll shower him with so much attention, I'll be able to give you that little brother or sister you deserve," Londyn promised nuzzling her nose against her beloved son.

"Sorry I'm late!" Londyn announced when she arrived at The Belvedere. She placed the baby carrier on the chair, then hugged Misty. "I've been craving some Mediterranean food, so I was excited when you told me this was where we were having lunch."

"No apology necessary. I'm just happy I can spend some time with you and the little one." She moved the blanket to see a sleeping Easton. "He's such a cutie," Misty gushed.

"He is." She gazed at her son lovingly. "If you would've told me two years ago my life was going to revolve around a baby, I would've said you were insane. Now, I'm plotting on baby number two," Londyn laughed.

"Wow, so soon?"

"If I had my way...yes. Sterling prefers we wait. I think he's feeling neglected. But he's finally getting his wish. The reason I was late, I had interviews with some potential nannies. I found the perfect one. She was referred by Sterling's business partner Kash. Her name is Angela, and she starts tomorrow. This will free up some time to spend with my hubby."

"And perhaps get back to work. Before you protest," Misty added, noticing Londyn shifting in her chair, "Just hear me out."

"Is that why you invited me to lunch...to discuss business?" she cut her eyes at Misty.

"Of course, I wanted to see you and my God-son, but a role did come across my desk, and immediately I thought of you. Honestly, I wasn't even sure you were ready because last time I saw you, you were still holding on to some baby weight."

"I'm going to try to not be offended by your comment."

"You shouldn't," Misty insisted. "This particular role calls for the woman to be in great shape."

"Well, I still need to put in some more work in the gym before I would consider myself to be in great shape."

"Trust me, that body is on point," Misty nodded in approval. "What you're wearing shows you've lost all your baby weight." Misty complimented Londyn on how she looked in the sleeveless nude snakeskin print corset top and high rise vintage blue wash skinny jeans with a raw hemline finish.

"Thank you. Your compliments are appreciated," Londyn winked.

"It's all true. Yes, I'm your friend, but remember I'm also your agent. I wouldn't send you out to audition for a role that I didn't believe you could make your own. With that being said, will you at least read over the script?" Misty reached in her coated canvas tote. Placing the screenplay on the table.

"I promise to read it over, but I don't think I'm ready to be away from Easton for long stretches of time to film a movie."

"That's the beautiful part, the majority of the movie is being filmed right here in LA."

"This might actually be doable," Londyn said scanning through the pages.

"Once you read it, I'm convinced you'll be hooked. But no pressure."

"Oh please, there is always pressure when it comes to you," Londyn laughed, "but maybe dabbling in work is what I need."

"It's obvious being a wife and mother is fulfilling because you're truly glowing. I've never seen you look so radiant. But..."

"I knew a but was coming," Londyn hissed interrupting Misty.

"All I was going to say was although you have this fairytale marriage, I don't want you to give up on your own career. You were an in demand working actress. I don't think you should give up on your dreams because they're still within your reach."

"This is why you're the best agent and also a dear friend. You always know how to give me

that push when I need it, put things in perspec-
tive and most importantly, remind me how vital
it is to stay true to myself. Thank you for that,"
Londyn smiled warmly. "Now enough of this,
let's eat!"

Londyn stood in front of the mirror inspecting
herself in the lavender one-piece lace baby doll
with cutout front keyhole detail and matching
panties. This was the fourth piece of lingerie she
tried on and still couldn't decide which one to
wear. Londyn wanted tonight to be perfect, and
it started with what was draping her body.

After her lunch with Misty, Londyn decided
to stop at Luxe Lingerie on N. Camden Dr. to pick
up several items. She wanted to surprise Sterling with a romantic evening and of course that
meant sexy lingerie. In her mind they had a lot to
celebrate, finally finding a nanny for Easton and
getting back to her other love—acting.

"This is the one!" Londyn determined ex-
citedly when she slipped on the blush lace ted-
dy with the center bow and the back cutout. Her

decision came right on time because she heard Sterling coming up the stairs. She placed herself in the center of the bed with the Olde World 60" Swarovski Element chandelier casting a soft il-luminating glow down on her body. There were well placed Jo Loves Pomelo candles around the bedroom making for an inviting ambience.

"What's all this?" Sterling's eyes moved smoothly throughout the room, observing every detail until relaxing his gaze upon his wife.

"Welcome home, baby," Londyn smiled se-ductively. "I feel like lately I haven't shown you how much I adore you."

"Really?" Sterling had that cunning smirk on his face like he was up to no good and she wel-comed it. He began taking off his suit, tie and unbuttoning his shirt before reaching the bed. She admired every inch of her husband's sculpt-ed frame, and he showed her he desired her just the same. Gently spreading her thighs with his strong arms, he glided his magical tongue down her body, licking his way between her legs. Each lick to the clit had Londyn quivering with delight. Sterling paused for a moment, and she begged him not to stop.

"You feel too damn good. Please don't stop," she pleaded. His gifted tongue returned to her hot spot soon bringing her to an all-consuming endless orgasm. Not interrupting the pleasure, he was on top of her, moving smoothly causing Londyn to moan deeply in the back of her throat. From the very first time they made love, they were in perfect rhythm, riding a wave they had created and unified them as one.

# Chapter Six

## *Bring Me Down*

"What do you mean you're going back to work?" Sterling initially thought he misunderstood Londyn because she was very casual with her approach.

"I mentioned last week I was considering it."

"No, you said a couple weeks ago when you were out to lunch with Misty, she gave you a script to read and asked for your feedback."

"Right, and once I read it, I thought there was a part that was perfect for me," she said eagerly, taking a bite of her vegetable omelette. They were outside on the terrace enjoying breakfast

and Londyn thought this was the perfect opportunity to give her husband the exciting news, but
he didn't quite view it that way.

"Why are you going back to work?" Sterling
questioned placing the newspaper he was reading on the table.

"I think it's the right time. We finally found
the perfect nanny who is wonderful with Easton.
We've been spending a lot of time together and I
feel like our marriage is the best it's ever been."

"So why would you want to disrupt that by
going back to a career that you don't need."

"I'm not sure what you mean by that." Londyn was perplexed by the statement.

"You have access to more than enough money to get whatever you want, so again why do
you need to go back to work? Getting a nanny for
Easton, was to enable you to be more available
to me. Not to free up time so you can chase some
frivolous dream."

"Is that what you think of my acting career,"
she said feeling hurt by her husband's callous
comment.

"It's not what I think, it's an observation. You
just stated our marriage is the best it's ever been.
Don't you want to keep it that way?"

"Of course, I do," Londyn uttered stroking

the side of Sterling's well-defined face. "And I will. I promise not to let dabbling in acting again interfere with my time with you and our family. You'll always come first. It would just be nice to have something else in my life that I enjoy doing. Please tell me this won't be a problem for you."

"It won't be a problem as long as you keep your word. Which means this movie thing you're doing, won't affect your obligations to me as my wife."

"It won't, I promise."

Sterling went back to reading his newspaper leaving Londyn uneasy about the decision she made. Before she could dwell on it any further, she saw Jayla floating through the living room, bubbly as always.

"Good morning to my beautiful sister," she cheered giving Londyn a hug. "And my handsome brother-in-law."

"Hello gorgeous!" Londyn beamed thrilled to have her little sister living with them.

"Good day," Sterling said dryly, briefly look-ing up to acknowledge Jayla's presence.

"You look so cute in that outfit!!" Londyn loved how the pink terry cloth short set with the crop top, adjustable spaghetti straps, V-neck and tie back, looked on Jayla's petite frame. "What do you have planned today?"

"I'm actually about to go hang out with Angela and Easton at the park," she said taking a bite of one of Londyn's strawberries.

"I think it's great you and Jayla get along so well. You all have become fast friends. It's really nice, don't you think babe?"

"Sure," Sterling said with indifference.

"Well, I'm sure they're ready to go. Later on tonight me and Jayla are going out for drinks with Ryan. He said there was this cute new lounge he wanted to take us to," Jayla said taking one more strawberry before making her exit.

"Well have fun and call me if you need me!" Londyn called out. "Moving to LA has really turned out to be the best decision for Jayla. In a very short period of time, she has really blossomed. I haven't seen her this upbeat since before our father passed away."

"Baby, if you're happy then I'm happy. I know how much you love your sister and if having her here puts a smile on your face, then she can stay for as long as you like."

"I feel so lucky to have you," Londyn smiled warmly.

"Because you are, as I am also lucky to have you."

"I guess that makes us two lucky people," she moved closer sharing an intimate kiss with her husband. Just looking at him got Londyn wet.

"Sorry to bother you all," Angela said coming outside on the terrace.

"Don't be silly. The woman who takes care of our precious son could never be a bother. Isn't that right baby?" Londyn glanced over at Sterling

"Absolutely," he agreed.

"I just wanted to let you know that I'm about to take Easton to the park with Jayla."

"Yeah, she stopped by a little while ago and mentioned that. You all have fun and send me a couple pics of our handsome son," Londyn requested.

"Will do," Angela said waving goodbye.

"Babe, we are home alone. I think we should celebrate," Londyn teased, undressing her husband with her eyes. He put his newspaper down and she crawled on top of his lap as he slid her panties to the side. His thick dick penetrated deep inside her walls as they made love with the sun and cool morning breeze as their backdrop.

***Three Months Later...***

"Cut!" the director yelled as they wrapped up the scene before taking a lunch break. Londyn headed to her dressing room anxious to call Misty.

"Do you have any news?" she asked before Misty could even get out a proper hello.

"Good afternoon is always a great conversation starter," Misty countered. "I heard you're doing excellent on the movie set, it's like you haven't missed a beat since you've been gone."

"Yep, we're wrapping the movie up this week. But is this what we're doing. Dancing around every topic except the one I called you about," Londyn popped.

"Girl, let me enjoy messing with you. You were off the scene for a minute," Misty kidded.

"Fine, get it out of your system so you can hurry up and get back to business."

"Dang, now that you're a mother bear, you take away all the fun."

"Speaking of being a mother bear, let me check on Easton. He should be taking his nap. Seeing him look so sweet while sleeping will help me get through the rest of my day on set."

"You can actually see my Godson from your dressing room?"

"Sure can. You know how technology is today. But I can't take credit, it was actually Kash's idea," Londyn admitted. "I installed a camera in Easton's bedroom. Now I can be with him even when I'm not home," Londyn bragged, pulling up the app up on her iPad.

"Let's pivot away from mommy talk for one second and discuss business. When you called me, I was just getting off the phone with the casting director. Everyone loved your audition You got the part!" Misty informed her, thrilled to give Londyn the exciting news.

"I have to go!" Londyn suddenly shouted, abruptly ending the call leaving Misty dumbfounded.

Londyn didn't even bother waiting for her driver to come pick her up. This was an emergency. One of the on-set assistants was more than happy to let the star of the movie borrow her car. She even offered to drive Londyn wherever she needed to go but this was a ride she wanted to take alone. She sped to their Holmby Hills estate as if there wasn't a single cop on duty. Londyn kicked off her six-inch heels and sprinted up the staircase and ran down the winding hallway until she reached Easton's bedroom.

"Mrs. Pierce, I wasn't expecting you home so early," Angela said cradling Easton.

"Put my son down in his bed."

"He just woke up. I was about to feed him."

"He'll be fine. Now put my son down," Londyn demanded.

"Sure," Angela said, doing as she was told. "Is there something wrong? You seem upset," she remarked after making sure Easton was comfortable in his crib.

"How long have you been fuckin' my husband Angela?"

"Excuse me?" the nanny sounded offended by the question. "I'm not! Why would you even think such a thing?"

"Cut the bullshit you fuckin' hussy. I saw you sucking his dick on camera, right here in this very room where my son was sleeping. Now answer my question before I drag your ass through this whole fuckin' house!" Londyn threatened.

"Mrs. Pierce, it's not what you think," Angela said becoming emotional.

"Stop with the theatrics because I'm the only

actress in this room. I'm going to ask you one last time, how long have you been fuckin' my husband?"

"For the last two months," Angela disclosed.

"Have you fucked in our bed?"

"Yes," she nodded. "I'm sorry."

"No, the fuck you're not. Just get out of my house...NOW!!" she belted in a powerful tone that seemed to make the room vibrate.

Angela grabbed a few of her items and was walking out the bedroom before breaking her stride and stopping mid step. "Mrs. Pierce, I really have a great deal of respect for you, so I feel compelled to let you know that I'm not the only woman your husband is seeing."

"What do you mean, you're not the only woman?"

"He's been seeing Jayla too."

"You lying bitch!" Londyn leaped at Angela, ready to put her fist through her mouth, but she stopped herself thinking of the hefty lawsuit the lowdown tramp would file against her if she laid hands.

"I know you must hate me, but I have no reason to lie to you about this. Jayla confided in me a couple weeks ago while we were out having lunch. She swore me to secrecy. Your sister loves you but just like I did, she succumbed to Sterling's charms. Jayla thinks she's in love with your husband."

"Get out! GET OUT!" Londyn screamed out in the most gut-wrenching pain. She dropped to her knees wishing she could delete this entire day out of her memory forever.

# Chapter Seven

## *Remorse*

"My fuckin' sister Sterling! My sister!" Londyn screamed before he even got through the ornate wrought-iron front doors."

"Londyn, what are you yelling about? You need to calm down," he said remaining composed although his wife was in full rage mode.

"Calm down! I find out you've been having sex with my sister, and you think I'm going to calm down. You're lucky I didn't come to your office and burn the fuckin' building down!" she exploded.

"Have you lost your mind? Why in the world would you think I'd have sex with your sister?"

he asked belligerently. "I would never cheat on you, and I'd definitely not cheat on you with Jayla," he vehemently denied.

"Amazing," Londyn scoffed, facing the bridal staircase. She tilted her head up at the double-height entry foyer displaying a chandelier dangling from the sky-lit ceiling, which she remained fixated on for a few seconds.

"Baby, I don't know where this nonsense is coming from, but I love you. I would never betray you or do anything to destroy our family. I can promise you that," Sterling vowed, wrapping his strong arms around his wife.

"Get yo' muthafuckin' arms off me!" she spit pushing her husband away. "It's amazing to me that I never knew that you can lie as easy as you breathe. Are you going to deny fuckin' the nanny too?"

Sterling didn't flinch. Remaining committed to his initial stance of being a monogamous husband. If this was a game of poker, he would win but fortunately Londyn knew what cards he had been dealt.

"You lying sonofabitch, I saw you! Earlier today, you were getting your dick sucked by Angela in our son's bedroom. And don't bother denying it, I have you on tape."

It was only then, when that bit of information was revealed did Sterling's hardened exterior begin to crack. He folded his hands and pressed them against his mouth closing his eyes for a moment. He was contemplating what lie he could tell to explain everything away but there was none. He was caught and all Sterling could do was beg for his wife's forgiveness but instead he chose a different approach.

"I told you not to go back to work. There was no need for you to start taking those bullshit acting gigs again," he griped. "You don't need the money. It was a waste of your time and kept you away from me. What did you expect me to do? I'm a man and I have needs."

"So, you're blaming me because you chose to stick your dick in our son's nanny and my sister. This is classic."

"Londyn, I fucked up and got involved with Angela, but I never had sex with Jayla. I need you to get past this indiscretion."

"That will never happen. I'm done with you."

"You're done...what the hell does that mean?"

"It means I want a divorce. I will never stay married to a man who can rip my heart out and step all over it with such malice. You disgust me!" Londyn turned to walk away and didn't notice Sterling charging towards her until he had her pinned up against the wall with his hand wrapped around her neck.

"You will never divorce me. It's till death do us part," he warned in a haunting deep voice mounting pressure on her throat, restricting her air. He continued to throttle Londyn until he felt she reached her brink.

Cutting off the flow of oxygen to her brain had Londyn gasping for air once Sterling stopped compressing her neck so tightly. She feared she was on the verge of unconsciousness when her husband impaired her breathing. For a moment it seemed he had no intent of letting go.

"You tried to kill me, you sick fuck," her words fluttered heavily.

"I don't try to do things; I make them happen. So no, I did not try to kill you because if that's what I wanted, you would be dead."

Londyn had her hand on her neck trying to regain her composure, while at the same time staring at a man she no longer recognized. This person standing a few feet away couldn't be her husband and the father of the beautiful child she gave birth to only a year ago. Sterling Pierce wasn't the man she had fell deeply in love with, he was a monster.

Sterling leaned back in his chair within the confines of his office lost in his thoughts. He was replaying what transpired between him and Londyn. He was a fixer and was strategizing how to fix his marriage when his contemplating was interrupted by a knock at his office door.

"Do you have a minute?" Kash asked pushing the door open. "I wanted to go over this month's financial report before the board meeting later on this afternoon."

"Can we go over it in about an hour? I have some things I'm dealing with right now," Sterling said taking a call from his assistant. "Did you take care of that for me?"

"Yes. A truck full of flowers have already been delivered to the house and I just received confirmation that the jewelry will arrive within an hour."

"Make sure you notify me when Londyn receives it."

"Will do."

"Thanks Allison," Sterling said ending the call.

"Is everything okay with Londyn?" Kash inquired.

"No, but I'm working to rectify the situation."

"What happened?" Kash stepped back to close the office door but was stopped when he noticed someone headed in his direction and the receptionist trailing behind him.

"You can't go in there!" she screamed but the man ignored her, instead speeding up his pace.

"Can I help you?" Kash stepped forward blocking the man's path.

"I'm so sorry Mr. Pierce," Valerie whined. "I tried to stop him, but he wouldn't listen."

Sterling stood up and came from behind his desk. The man used the opportunity to duck around Kash and go directly to the source. "Sterling Pierce, you've been served!" the man announced and then disappeared as hastily as he arrived.

Sterling opened the large envelope and promptly noticed the law firm on the legal documents. He immediately picked up the phone and called his wife, but she didn't answer. He called her back multiple times with the same results, and he became infuriated. "FUCK!!" he roared, ripping the phone out the wall and tossing it across the room.

"Man, what is the deal?" Kash questioned with concern. "Valerie, can you give us a minute."

"Of course," she said closing the office door.

"Sterling, talk to me. We've been best friends since attending Harvard together and now we're business partners. You know you can tell me anything. What's going on with you and your wife?"

"I really fucked up." Sterling spoke in a low and collected tone. Then like a light switch he flipped from calmness back to rage, grabbing the first thing within his reach, he started slamming his laptop on the desk.

Sterling's explosive temper came as no surprise to Kash, but he was more interested in what had set him off. "Man, try to relax and tell me what is going on with you."

"Londyn just served me with divorce papers and a restraining order," Sterling disclosed tossing the documents on the floor. "Now she's not taking my calls. I need to go home and talk some sense into her," he fumed grabbing his keys to leave.

"What the fuck are you doing? You just said you were served with a restraining order. If you go home, you'll be arrested," Kash warned, picking up the legal documents and reading over them.

"So, what...I can't go in my own fuckin' house or see my own son! I'll never let that happen."

Sterling was pacing the floor in his office, looking for something else to smash.

"You need to speak with one of our internal attorneys and immediately retain a family lawyer. Until then stay away from Londyn," Kash advised. "Now tell me what the fuck happened between the two of you."

Sterling sat back down in his chair letting out a deep sigh. "I got caught cheating," he admitted.

"I thought you ended things with Valerie?"

"I did. I stopped fucking Valerie shortly after I met Londyn."

"Then who?" Kash waited for an answer.

"The nanny."

"You can't be serious," Kash shook his head. "Why are you fuckin' another woman where you lay your head at?"

"I know but I got caught slipping. Londyn went back to work and every time I would come home, there Angela would be walking around half naked, basically throwing the pussy at me. I finally took a bite of the apple," Sterling swallowed hard.

"I get it but damn man," Kash sighed. "Fire Angela, if Londyn hasn't done so already. Explain to your wife that you messed up and it will never happen again. After begging for forgiveness, Londyn might take you back."

"If only it was that simple. For some reason she thinks I'm fuckin' her sister too."

"Jayla! You fucked Jayla! You're doing way too much. You're lucky she only served you with divorce papers and a restraining order and not a bullet to the head. Wait—did you really strangle Londyn?" Kash asked reading over all the details.

"I didn't fuck Jayla. But I did strangle Londyn," he acknowledged. "I was angry when she said she wanted a divorce. I didn't want to lose my family. I had to stop her but obviously I failed because everything is slipping away," Sterling's voice trailed off sounding defeated.

"No doubt you fucked up, to the point your marriage is more than likely over, because I don't think Londyn will ever forgive you. But luckily you had her sign a prenup, so *everything* isn't slipping away," Kash said trying to put a positive spin on a disastrous situation.

"The thing is, I never got around to having Londyn sign a prenup or a postnup," he revealed. "We got married in Vegas, soon after she was pregnant with my son. I believed we would be together for the rest of our lives."

"So, if you get a divorce, Londyn will own a

percentage of our Venture Capital Firm...this is some bullshit," Kash fumed.

"It won't come to that. Londyn is not leaving me. I'm going to make things right and keep our family together. We will never divorce," Sterling promised.

# Chapter Eight

## *On My Own*

"Jayla is still not answering her phone! Where the fuck is she!" Londyn yelled slamming the kitchen cabinet. Misty and Ryan watched as she poured herself a glass of wine while fussing about her sister's whereabouts.

"Were you able to get in touch with your mother?" Misty asked hating to see Londyn on edge.

"Yes, and she hasn't spoken to Jayla in the last few days. Maybe Sterling warned her that I knew they had been fuckin' around and got her out of town, so I couldn't slap the shit out of her,"

Londyn said breathing heavy, pouring herself another drink.

"I still can't believe Jayla did some fucked up shit like that," Ryan said outraged.

"Maybe she didn't. I think we should hold off judgement until Jayla has a chance to tell her side of the story," Misty suggested.

"I hear you, but why would the nanny lie on Jayla? They were cool wit' each other. The three of us even hung out a few times. All I'm sayin' is she needs to explain herself, cause this ain't makin' sense," Ryan said firmly, folding his arms.

"Exactly! I've left numerous voice and text messages and she hasn't responded. If my sister had nothing to hide, why is she suddenly ghost," Londyn said scornfully. "You would think you would want to defend yourself if you were accused of fuckin' your sister's husband."

"I'll admit, it doesn't look good for Jayla," Misty sighed sadly. "I guess I'm just hoping for your sake Londyn, it isn't true. You're going through a lot right now. You had to get rid of your nanny, husband and maybe your sister all at the same damn time. It's too much. And I have to ask, are you sure you want to move forward with a divorce? Is it truly over between you and Sterling?"

"Yes." Londyn answered without hesitation.

"I don't care how many times he floods this house with flowers, or how much he spends on jewelry, I'm done. I loved and honestly still love Sterling, but our marriage is over. It'll be hard but thank God I have Easton and of course you and Ryan."

"You know I always got yo' back, that will never change," Ryan said ferociously protective of his friend.

"As do I but I'm worried about you Londyn. Not only is this entire situation emotionally draining, but Sterling also almost killed you."

"I still can't believe that snake ass nigga put his hands on you. He needs his ass beat," Ryan boiled.

"There is a restraining order in place, and Sterling knows he will be arrested if he comes anywhere near me. He has too much to lose. He doesn't want to take a chance and destroy his reputation with an ugly divorce."

"I hear you, but I would feel more comfortable if you and Easton weren't here alone. Why don't you let me stay with you until things calm down," Misty proposed.

"I think that's a good idea," Ryan agreed. "I can stay here too if you like."

"You two are the best! That would be perfect," she smiled warmly, giving them both a hug.

Londyn did welcome their company. She was trying to be strong but not only was she angry, but
her heart had been broken and she wasn't sure if
it would ever be healed.

Kash's dick was plunging into her soaking wet
pussy as he squeezed her titties, hitting it from
the back. She was biting down on her lip, moaning
as the pounding became more aggressive. There
was a mixture of pain and pleasure as she took
the dick down. Kash was gripping on her ass
while her swollen lips tightened around his thick
tool.

"Fuck!" she howled with her head buried
in the pillow. Her legs began shaking feeling his
dick throb with each thrust as he inched closer to
being ready to cum and she was reaching her cli-
max. Kash did two more powerful pumps before
grunting loudly and collapsing.

"Damn, that shit felt fuckin' good," he moaned
laying on his back before lighting up a blunt.

"Let me get a hit," Angela said also feeling
sexually satisfied.

"I had that pussy gushing," Kash joked, passing the blunt to her. "Did you get that wet for Sterling?"

"Honestly that nigga pretty much only wanted head. He was selfish with the dick," Angela cracked. "So selfish that at first, I didn't think your plan was going to work," she said bringing the blunt to her lips and taking a few short puffs before slowly drawing in her desired amount of smoke and breathing in deeper through her diaphragm and exhaling. "I had to practically shove the pussy in his face. I was ready to give up," she laughed.

"I remember. I had to sweeten the deal because you were no longer motivated. But your diligence paid off. Londyn has filed for divorce, and she got a restraining order. Pretty soon Sterling will be left with nothing. I'll have his family and complete control over the business."

"Don't be so quick to count Sterling out. He has a way with women. Londyn might forgive him. I've seen them together, they're deeply in love."

"I wouldn't be so confident if you hadn't told Londyn that Sterling was also fuckin' her sister. I don't care how much they're in love, she will never take him back after that."

"I still don't understand why you had me tell her that lie. Once she speaks to Jayla and finds out it isn't true, the damage will be undone, and more than likely Londyn will forgive her husband and your plan will be a bust," Angela shrugged.

"That's why you're a worker and I'm the boss because I know how to get shit done," Kash boasted, getting out the bed.

"What does that mean?" Angela sat up, pulling the flat sheet over her exposed breasts.

"It means that Jayla will never have an opportunity to deny your claims. If anything, she will confirm them." Kash gave a devilish grin and disappeared into the bathroom to take a shower leaving Angela try to make sense of the unexplainable.

# Chapter Nine

## *Over My Dead Body*

Londyn pulled into the parking lot looking forward to a day at the spa. It was the perfect place to get centered, which is what she needed. For the last few weeks, she had been full of anxiety, unable to sleep and basically stressed the fuck out. She was yearning for the calming sea salt body scrub with almond oil and lavender, an aromatic milk bath with Japanese camelia oil and oat extract, a relaxing massage to soothe her body muscles and finally a 30-minute sleep under a luxury weighted blanket to help increase serotonin production. This would be Londyn's reset and rejuvenate moment to melt away stress.

"Note to self to do something super special for Misty for booking this spa appointment," Londyn mouthed out loud, grabbing her purse before stepping out her SUV.

"How long did you think you would be able to keep me away." Sterling spoke in a menacing tone, mounting Londyn against the driver side door.

"Get away from me Sterling! You know you're not supposed to be anywhere near me. You're in violation of a restraining order."

"I guess you haven't spoken with your lawyer. My attorney got that restraining order dismissed. You will not keep me away from my son and I will be moving back home tonight."

"It doesn't matter because we're still getting a divorce. Our marriage is over!" Londyn barked shoving Sterling in an attempt to get him out her space, but she was no match for his athletic build, as he barely moved.

"I still love you Londyn and I know you still love me too. Even with everything that's happened in the last few weeks I believe we can salvage our marriage. I apologize for the infidelity and putting my hands on you, and I promise to try to do better. I'm also willing to forgive you and put that behind us."

"You are truly a narcissist fuck! What do you need to forgive me for as I haven't done a mutha-fuckin' thing wrong," she fussed, ready to punch Sterling in his face.

"I see your still on your bullshit," his anger continued flaring up.

"The only bullshit is coming from you. And where is my sister? Has she been keeping you company while we've been apart, or has it been Angela?" Londyn ranted, jabbing her finger in his chest.

"I told you, I never fucked Jayla! There's more than enough available pussy in LA that I don't have to screw your sister. And I haven't seen nor talked to Angela."

"Whatever Sterling. I don't believe anything you say. Now move the fuck out of my way!" she demanded.

"I'll be home tonight, Londyn."

"Then I'll be leaving and I'm taking Easton with me."

"You're not taking my son anywhere."

"Oh yes, I am. We're not living under the same roof with you."

"Londyn, I'm going to tell you one last time, I want to save our marriage. But if you force the issue and move forward with a divorce, you will live to regret it. I'm not the type of man you want to go to war with because I will destroy you and get sole custody of my son in the process," Sterling warned.

"Are you threatening me, you piece of shit!"

"Just making you mindful of what the consequences of your choices will be," Sterling cautioned as he constricted Londyn's arms, peering deep into her eyes with an ominous glare.

"You will never take Easton away from me. Over my dead body," she spit full of furry.

"That can be arranged," he said releasing her from his grasp.

Londyn rushed off never looking back. The line had been drawn and the war between Pierce v. Pierce had officially begun.

"Here she comes now," Misty said to the police officers when she saw Londyn pulling up to the front of the house. "I've been trying to call you, but your phone kept going straight to voicemail," she called out to Londyn.

"My battery died, and I didn't have my phone charger," Londyn explained. "What's going on...why are these police officers here?" she was guarded believing the police presence had something to do with her husband.

"Mrs. Pierce, it's about your sister Jayla Lewis."

"What about Jayla?"

"Your sister has died. We're sorry to deliver this devastating news..." before he could finish, Londyn's legs went weak, and she fell to the ground. It happened so quickly that Misty nor the police officers had a chance to catch her fall. When she arrived home, a death notification was not the news Londyn had been expecting and within a matter of seconds her life had forever changed.

"Valerie, get my attorney on the phone!" Sterling yelled walking past her desk on the way to his office. He was about to slam the door, but Kash came in right behind him.

"Is everything okay?" he asked sounding as

if he was genuinely worried. "I heard you telling Valerie to get your attorney on the phone. Has something happened between you and Londyn?"

"What hasn't happened," Sterling grumbled. "I figured once my attorney got this restraining order lifted by the court, things could go back to normal."

"I didn't realize you got the restraining order dropped." That was the last thing Kash wanted. He needed to keep the once very much in love couple far apart.

"Yes. I hired an attorney someone in our legal department recommended and she's a beast."

"Great. So have you been in touch with Londyn...is there a chance you all will reconcile?" Kash was digging for all the dirt.

"That was the plan but after my confrontation with her earlier today, that's not going to happen. She's determined to move forward with the divorce. And I think part of the reason is because Londyn still believes I was fucking her sister. I don't understand why Jayla hasn't cleared that bullshit up. I even tried to get her on the phone to find out who put this mess in my wife's head but no luck."

"So, what are you going to do? Have you decided your next move?"

"I'm going to do what I do best. Annihilate the competition, which in this situation is my beautiful wife. I'm going to start with filing for sole custody of our son."

"I think that's a good idea. If Londyn wants to fight dirty, then you need to do the same. Pull out all the stops," Kash said encouraging Sterling. He was hoping for an all-out war.

"Mr. Pierce, I have your attorney on the phone," Valerie alerted him.

"Thanks...Kash, give me some privacy," Sterling said gesturing him to leave his office.

"Of course. We'll talk later."

Kash closed Sterling's office door with a smile spread across his face. Everything was working out the way he planned. He felt it was time to make his move on Londyn, because he assumed she had to be feeling vulnerable and wanted to use that vulnerability to his advantage.

# Chapter Ten

## *Justice For Jayla*

Angela watched as Londyn left Kash's home and got into her SUV. She pressed the start button on her car and began following behind her, making sure to keep enough distance to go unnoticed. When Londyn made a stop at a popular bakery, she was going to use that opportunity to make her move. Once Angela heard about Jayla's death, she had been determined to speak with Londyn, but to her surprise, Kash had been glued to her side. It appeared he was getting everything he wanted but Angela was resolute on making sure that never happened.

"Londyn, I need to speak with you," Angela called out, before she had a chance to get in her vehicle. Londyn turned around recognizing the familiar voice.

"What the hell are you doing here...are you following me?" Londyn put the bag of goodies she'd just purchased from the bakery on the passenger seat and then slammed the door. She faced Angela in a fighting stance. "What do you want?"

"I know I'm the last person you want to see or have a conversation with, but what I have to tell you is extremely important."

"Let me guess, Sterling has cut you off financially and now you're willing to testify on my behalf at the divorce hearing? Hmmm...hoping if you agree to tell the judge about your affair with my soon to be ex-husband, I'll cut you a check. Does that sound about right." Londyn chastised.

"No, it's not right. This is about Jayla."

"Don't you dare speak my sister's name!" Londyn stepped forward, stopping herself from lunging at Angela. "You telling me about her affair with Sterling is what pushed her to commit suicide. She couldn't live with the guilt of me knowing what she had done. You should've kept your mouth shut. You fuckin' my husband was enough betrayal for me to end my marriage."

"Kash felt differently," Angela blurted out. Giving Londyn no option other than to listen to what she had to say. "He wasn't confident that your husband having sex with me would be enough to end your marriage."

"Kash—what does Kash have to do with any of this? Answer me!"

Angela wanted Londyn's full attention, now she had it. "Kash is the one who told me to tell you that your husband was also having sex with Jayla. I didn't understand why he had me do that at first, but when I finally asked him, he said it was because that was the one thing you would never forgive Sterling for. Kash clearly knows your limit because he was right."

Londyn thought she was going to vomit. She wanted to curse Angela out and call her a lying bitch but, in her gut, she knew it was all true.

"Why?" was all Londyn could manage to say.

"He wanted Sterling's life, his wife and anything else he could take from him."

"That's it? Kash has wreaked havoc on my entire life because he is jealous of his best friend?" her heart was racing with vehemence consuming her spirit.

"You can add greed as he wanted to be the

sole owner of their company. Kash had also grown to hate Sterling. He felt he didn't deserve any of his success. He told me several times that Sterling didn't deserve you either and you should be his wife."

"Why are you telling me all this now?" Londyn wanted to know.

"Because I cared about Jayla, and I don't believe for a second she committed suicide."

"But she left a note. I know my sister's handwriting and she did write that letter. She admitted to her affair with Sterling and begged for my forgiveness," Londyn revealed, with her eyes tearing up.

"I guarantee you; your sister was forced to write that letter before she was murdered. When I told Kash that once you spoke with Jayla and realized Sterling never had sex with her, you all would probably reconcile. You know what he said, it would never happen because Jayla would confirm that what I told you was true. At the time, I didn't understand what Kash meant because I knew I told you an outright lie, but he was so confident and smug. Now I know why. Jayla had probably already been forced to write that suicide note and Kash knew she was dead or would be very soon." Angela's voiced cracked, as she was now the one holding back tears.

"This is the sickest shit I've ever heard in my life. I don't know who disgusts me more, Sterling or Kash," Londyn shook her head repulsed by what she had learned. "How long has Kash been orchestrating all this?"

"As you know he was the one that recommended me for the nanny position."

"So, wait, when I hired you Kash's plan had been set in motion?"

"Yes. When he had me apply for the nanny position, my only objective was to seduce your husband and make sure you found out," Angela made clear.

"That sonofabitch, he's been playing me this entire time." Londyn was becoming angrier by the minute realizing that Kash was a puppet master, pulling strings and using everyone around him to get what he wanted. "Kash was the one who told me to put the camera in Easton's bedroom, as if he was being a good friend. He said that although he heard you were a highly qualified nanny, to be on the safe side I should install the camera to make sure you were treating Easton with love and care. The nerve of that man." Londyn was biting down on her lip, she wanted to put a hurting on Kash bad.

"Why do you think you caught my performance, because Kash told me about the camera. He is an extremely cunning man."

"I don't think cunning is a strong enough word. More like a sociopath," Londyn presumed.

"When I read that Jayla's death had been ruled a suicide, I wanted to go to the police and tell them everything I knew. But I realized it would be my word against his. It's not like I have any evidence. Besides, once Kash found out I turned on him, I would be his next victim and would end up dead too. But I couldn't leave LA without you knowing the truth, Londyn. I know my apology probably means nothing to you but I'm truly sorry. I never knew when Kash hired me to seduce your husband, I would end up ruining so many lives," she said solemnly.

"This is not on you. The blame falls squarely on that sick fuck Kash."

"I wish there was a way to make him pay for what he did to Jayla, because she didn't deserve any of this. But there's nothing else I can do. Kash scares the hell out of me. I've been planning on getting out of town for several weeks now, but I couldn't leave until I spoke to you. Now that I have, I'm getting far away from this place. I'm going to start over somewhere else," Angela said with a sense of newfound purpose.

"I truly wish you well," Londyn said embracing Angela with an affectionate hug. "And thank you for coming to me with the truth. It took a lot of courage and I'm sincerely grateful."

'That wasn't the sendoff I was expecting, so thank you," Angela cried.

"No, *thank you*. And don't worry, Kash will pay dearly for every sin he's committed against me and mine. I will get justice for Jayla," Londyn promised.

# Chapter Eleven

## Destroy Myself Just For You

"Are we all in agreement that this is what we want to do?" Misty looked across the dining room table at Londyn and Ryan. They glanced at each other and nodded yes.

"Under the circumstances, this is the only plausible option for me. This will bring closure to all my problems while protecting me and my son. It must be done, and I thank you both for making it happen. None of this would be possible without you," Londyn stated full of gratitude.

After Angela revealed the harrowing truth, Londyn immediately shared every sordid detail with the two people she trusted most, Misty and Ryan. They were just as shocked and repulsed with the scheme Kash orchestrated. The three of them then made a collective decision to concoct their own scheme, spending the last several days going over every step on how to flawlessly execute their master plan.

"Since we are all in agreeance, it's time to implement the first step of the plan. Londyn, are you ready?" Misty asked.

"More than ready. I'm looking forward to it," she stated with confidence. "Ryan, I'll be in touch in a few hours when I'm ready for you to implement step two."

"I'll be waiting and ready," Ryan confirmed. The three of them each gave a high-five ready to get to work.

"Dinner was delicious." Londyn sat down next to Kash who was laying across the bed with his shirt off. She hated that before Angela told her the truth, she had fell for his lies and considered becoming serious with him once her divorce was finalized.

"Not as delicious as you," he said sprinkling kisses on her neck.

"Really...tell me how delicious I am," she smiled leaning her head back.

"I can't describe it with words, I need to show you."

"And I want you to, but we haven't opened that bottle of wine I brought over yet. The taste is so sweet. And after a glass or two it gives me this stimulating high that makes the sex that much better," she teased.

"Then let me go pop that shit open asap!" Kash jumped up from the bed and said.

"Baby, you already served me this magnificent dinner, now let me serve you. Lay down and relax."

Londyn went downstairs to the kitchen to pour their glasses of wine and spike Kash's drink. The only reason she was able to tolerate his touch was by reminding herself of the end results, and it would be well worth it.

"You know, I still can't believe you're my woman," Kash said proudly when she came back into his bedroom. He sat up in bed, taking the glass from Londyn.

"Believe it," she said leaning close, pressing her lips against his. "I didn't think I would find love again after my horrific ordeal with Sterling but here you are. Did you ever think we would be together?"

"If I could figure out how to get you away from my best friend," he remarked. "Do you know we both got introduced to you at the same time."

"Huh, I'm confused. I didn't meet you until after me and Sterling were married."

"I'm not talking about that. Me and Sterling were watching Love and Lies together, and you came across the movie screen. We both were instantly infatuated with you. A few years later when I got the call, and he told me he met and married you all within a few days, I wasn't surprised but I was mad."

"Why were you mad?"

"Because Sterling never deserved you. You were just another one of his trophies. Once he got you, you became part of his growing collection, and he took you for granted like he does everything else in his life."

"You're absolutely right. Hopefully this divorce will go in my favor, and I can put that chapter of my life behind me. I just pray he doesn't get custody of our son. I couldn't survive that."

"Londyn, don't worry I won't let that happen."

"But what can you do to help?"

"I know what Sterling loves more than anything—money. We launder millions of dollars for, let's just call them some unsavory people. I can get you certain paperwork that your attorney can use as a bargaining tool in the divorce. So, I promise you, I'll never let him take Easton."

"You would do that for me?"

"No doubt. Baby, I love you. These last couple months have been the best of my life."

"These last couple months have been life changing for me also. I'm so grateful you showed up that day at Jayla's memorial service. Dealing with her death, the divorce, I was at my breaking point, and you've been my rock ever since."

"And I will always be your rock," Kash said beginning to doze off as the drug Londyn put in his drink began to take effect.

"And I will always love you for that," she said kissing Kash one last time before he was knocked out. She tucked him in bed before grabbing his gun and keys so Ryan could execute the second part of their plan.

As promised, Ryan was waiting and ready when Londyn met up with him at the designated location. "Here you go," she said handing him the keys and gun.

"I have to ask you one last time, are you positive this is what you want to do?" Ryan waited for Londyn's confirmation. "Because after tonight there is no turning back."

"You mean after tonight; I'll be able to move forward," Londyn affirmed. "Because I have no interest in turning back. Now go make the magic happen."

"That's all I needed to hear," Ryan nodded, pumped about getting shit done.

Kash woke up to a loud pounding at his front door. He glanced at his phone, halfway sleep trying to see what time it was. He then scanned his bedroom remembering seeing Londyn's face and feeling her soft lips before closing his eyes.

"Damn, who the fuck can that be," he muttered when the pounding on his front door persisted. Kash headed downstairs and was stunned when he opened the door, and it seemed like the entire LAPD was staring back at him.

"Kash Nichols, you're under arrest for the murder of Sterling Pierce," they announced loudly, shaking him out of whatever stupor he had been in. He was now wide awake when the police placed the handcuffs around his wrists and escorted him to Los Angeles County Men's Central Jail to be booked for first degree murder.

*Epilogue...*

Londyn adjusted the strap on her ivory ruffle trimmed dress before sitting down in the chair facing Kash. There was a physical barrier separating them—a glass panel. They both picked up the phone at the same time.

"You have no idea how happy I am to see you," Kash said placing his hand on the glass.

"I'm happy to see you too my love." Londyn placed her hand over Kash's as if the glass was not separating them. "I'm sorry I couldn't come see you sooner, but things have been so crazy for me, especially with the police continuing their investigation into Sterling's murder."

"Did you have a chance to speak with them and confirm my alibi?" Kash wanted to know.

"I sat down with the police detectives yesterday with my attorney to answer their questions."

"Good," he said sounding relieved. "I'm ready to get out of this place. Now that you've told them everything like we discussed, they'll have no choice but to release me. I'll call my lawyer and let him know, so he can get on top of it."

"Kash, I don't think it's going to be that easy," Londyn said meekly.

"What do you mean...why do you say that?"

"I couldn't be your alibi. I had to tell them the truth because they threatened to charge me with accessory to murder and throw me in jail too."

"But that was just bullshit! Them trying to scare you. They don't have anything on you. Londyn, you need to go back in there and change your story. Tell the detectives you made a mistake. I need you to this for me—for us," he asserted.

"I'm sorry, what more do you want me to do. I did confirm we've been having an affair, and I was with you earlier that evening, but I had to leave and go home to my son. But they believe Sterling's murder happened later in the evening."

"Why the fuck would you tell them something like that?!" Kash seethed, putting his anger on display for Londyn while trying not to garner the attention of the guards.

"I didn't have a choice. I can't go to prison, especially now that I'm pregnant with your child."

"You're pregnant?" a glimpse of optimism

appeared in Kash's eyes.

"Yes. That's another reason I couldn't come see you sooner, I've been having morning sickness. At first, I thought I had a 24-hour stomach bug, but the vomiting persisted and I went to the doctor. Come to find out I'm carrying our child."

"I hope we have a daughter. She'll be beautiful just like her mother," Kash said lovingly.

Londyn smiled sweetly. "I hate I'll have to raise our child with you behind bars."

"I'll fight the charges because I didn't kill Sterling."

"I know you didn't, but the police have motive, because of our affair and you getting his share of the business, although now of course it's my share, since Sterling is dead."

"I still believe I can win. They can't even find the murder weapon. Their case is circumstantial with little to no evidence." Kash's determination was unwavering. "Then we can get married and raise our child together."

"Baby, I want that too and I'll do whatever I can to make it happen."

"Thank you for saying that because there is something I need for you to do."

"What is it?"

"I found out my bank accounts have been

frozen. The IRS started a money laundering investigation into my finances because of some bullshit anonymous tip they received. I haven't been able to get any further details and my attorney isn't much help. It's like anything that can go wrong is happening all at once," he fumed.

"Calm down. We'll get through this together. What do you need for me to do?"

"If I have any chance of winning at trial, I need a dream team of attorneys and that will cost a lot of money. Can you give me the money?" Kash asked.

"Of course. In exchange, I think you can sell me your share of the business. I mean, it is the fair thing to do. Don't you think?"

Londyn's request caught Kash off guard. He didn't realize this was going to be a give-and-take conversation. "My share of the company is worth millions and millions of dollars."

"I know but you're asking me to take money from my children, one of which will be your child, with no guarantee that the high price lawyers you hire will even beat the case. I would think you'd want to protect us and make sure our child received your share of the company in case anything happened to you."

"You're right. Baby, I'm sorry...I must sound

so selfish. I will sign over my share of the company to you. It's probably for the best since the IRS are investigating my personal finances. There is no reason for them to probe my business finances too."

"You're not being selfish. This is a difficult time for you...for both of us but we'll get through it—together. I have to go but I love," Londyn said blowing Kash a goodbye kiss. He didn't know it, but it would be the very last time she would come to visit him in prison.

Londyn walked out with her oversized matte black sunglasses shielding her face. "It worked," she told Misty closing the passenger side door of the car.

"He agreed to sell you his share of the company?"

"I mean did he really have a choice?" Londyn shrugged. "Once we called in that tip to the IRS and they froze his bank accounts, he was left strapped for cash. And you know he's desperate to pay for a dream team of lawyers. Of course, he asked his baby mama to help foot the bill," she laughed.

"Girl, you actually decided to use the I'm pregnant story?"

"You thought I was bullshitting?" Londyn

cracked. "You should've seen his eyes light up when he thought I would be doing his bid with him as a pregnant woman, waiting for him to get out of prison and come home to me." The women burst out laughing. "Honestly, I think that was the catalyst to him agreeing to sign over his share of the company. As if I would ever carry a baby that had his DNA."

"I wouldn't be surprised. His ego is on the same level as Sterling's was. He's probably convinced you are sincerely in love with him. Stupid fuck," Misty smacked.

"Stupid is right," Londyn rolled her eyes. "Did Ryan have a chance to place the murder weapon where I told him too?"

"Of course."

"Wait until the cops find the gun and inform Kash his weapon was used to kill his best friend. I think that will convince him to take a plea deal, opposed to rolling the dice at trial, being found guilty and receiving life with no possibility of parole," Londyn reasoned.

"I agree. I mean he's fucked either way. He needs to take the fuck that's a little less painful," Misty nodded.

"I don't care how Kash is fucked as long as he is out of my life. He ruined my marriage when he brought Angela into our lives. I wanted to spend the rest of my life with Sterling until I realized how dangerous he truly was. He should've never filed for sole custody of my son. Easton belongs with me, his mother. Not that sick fuck.

Now Sterling and Kash are both where they belong—one is dead and the other is in jail. Good riddance," she said as Misty put the top down on the AMG S63 and drove off, letting the California breeze intoxicate them. Londyn had no idea what the future held, but she was inspired to begin a new chapter in her life as a highly respected wealthy widow.

A KING PRODUCTION

# The Legacy

*Keep The Family Close...*

*A Novel*

# JOY DEJA KING

# Chapter One

## Raised By Wolves

"Alejo, we've been doing business for many years and my intention is for there to be many more. But I do have some concerns..."

"That's why we're meeting today," Alejo interjected, cutting Allen off. I've made you a very wealthy man. You've made millions and millions of dollars from my family..."

"And you've made that and much more from our family," Clayton snapped, this time being the one to cut Alejo off. "So let's acknowledge this being a mutual beneficial relationship between both of our families."

Alejo slit his eyes at Clayton, feeling disrespected, his anger rested upon him. Clayton was the youngest son of Allen Collins but also the most vocal. Alejo then turned towards his son Damacio who sat calmly not saying a word in his father's defense, which further enraged the dictator of the Hernandez family.

An ominous quietness engulfed the room as the Collins family remained seated on one side of the table and the Hernandez family occupied the other.

"I think we can agree that over the years we've created a successful business relationship that works for all parties involved," Kasir said, speaking up and trying to be the voice of reason and peacemaker for what was quickly turning into enemy territory. "No one wants to create new problems. We only want to fix the one we currently have so we can all move forward."

"Kasir, I've always liked you," Alejo said with a half smile. "You've continuously conducted yourself with class and respect. Others can learn a lot from you."

"Others, meaning your crooked ass nephews," Clayton barked not ignoring the jab Alejo was taking at him. He then pointed his finger at Felipe and Hector, making sure that everyone at the table knew exactly who he was speaking of since there were a dozen family members on the Hernandez side of the table.

Chaos quickly erupted within the Hernandez family as the members began having a heated exchange amongst each other. They were speaking Spanish and although neither Allen nor Clayton understood what was being said, Kasir spoke the language fluently.

"Dad, I think we need to fall back and not let this meeting get any further out of control. Let's table this discussion for a later date," Kasir told his father in a very low tone.

"Fuck that! We ain't tabling shit. As much money as we bring to this fuckin' table and these snakes want to short us. Nah, I ain't having it. That shit ends today," Clayton stated, not backing down.

"You come here and insult me and my family with your outrageous accusations," Alejo stood up and yelled, pushing back the single silver curl that kept falling over his forehead. "I will not tolerate such insults from the likes of you. My family does good business. You clearly cannot say the same."

"This is what you call good business," Clayton shot back, placing his iPhone on the center of the table. Then pressing play on the video that was sent to him.

Alejo grabbed the phone from off the table and watched the video intently, scrutinizing every detail. After he was satisfied he then handed it to his son Damacio, who after viewing, passed it around to the other family members at the table.

"What's on that video?" Kasir questioned his brother.

"I want to know the same thing," his father stated.

"Let's just say that not only are those two motherfuckers stealing from us, they're stealing from they own fuckin' family too," Clayton huffed, leaning back in his chair, pleased that he had the proof to back up his claims.

"We owe your family an apology," Damacio said, as his father sat back down in his chair with a glaze of defeat in his eyes. It was obvious the old man hated to be wrong and had no intentions of admitting it, so his son had to do it for him.

"Does that mean my concerns will be addressed and handled properly?" Allen Collins questioned.

"Of course. You have my word that this matter will be corrected in the very near future and there is no need for you to worry, as it won't happen again. Please accept my apology on behalf of my entire family," Damacio said, reaching over to shake each of their hands.

"Thank you, Damacio," Allen said giving a firm handshake. "I'll be in touch soon."

"Of course. Business will resume as usual and we look forward to it," Damacio made clear before the men gathered their belongings and began to make their exit.

"Wait!" shouted Alejo. The Collins men stopped in their tracks and turned towards him.

"Father, what are you doing?" Damacio asked, confused by his sudden outburst.

"There is something that needs to be addressed and no one is leaving this room until it's done," Alejo demanded.

With smooth ease, Clayton rested his arm towards the back of his pants, placing his hand on the Glock 20–10mm auto. Before the meeting, the Collins' men had agreed to have their security team wait outside in the parking lot instead of coming in the building, so it wouldn't be a hostile environment. But that didn't stop Clayton from taking his own precautions. He eyed his brother

Kasir who maintained his typical calm demeanor that annoyed the fuck out of Clayton.

"Alejo, what else needs to be said that wasn't already discussed?" Allen asked, showing no signs of distress.

"Please, come take a seat," Alejo said politely. Allen stared at Alejo then turned to his two sons and nodded his head as the three men walked back towards their chairs.

Alejo wasted no time and immediately began his over the top speech. "I was born in Mexico and raised by wolves. I was taught that you kill or be killed. When I rose to power by slaughtering my enemies and my friends, I felt no shame," Alejo stated, looking around at everyone sitting at the table. His son Damacio swallowed hard as his Adam's apple seemed to be throbbing out of his neck.

"As I got older and had my own family, I decided I didn't want that for my children. I wanted them to understand the importance of loyalty, honor, and respect," Alejo said proudly, speaking with his thick Spanish accent, which was heavier than usual. He moved away from his chair and began to pace the floor as he spoke. "Without understanding the meaning of being loyal, honoring, and respecting your family, you're worthless.

Family forgives but some things are unforgivable so you have no place on this earth or in my family."

Then, without warning and before anyone had even noticed, blood was squirting from Felipe's slit throat. With the same precision and quickness, Alejo took his sharp pocketknife and slit Hector's throat too. Everyone was too stunned and taken aback to stutter a word.

Alejo wiped the blood off his pocketknife on the white shirt that a now dead Felipe was wearing. He kept wiping until the knife was clean. "That is what happens when you are disloyal. It will not be tolerated...ever." Alejo made direct contact with each of his family members at the round table before focusing on Allen. "I want to personally apologize to you and your sons. I do not condone what Felipe and Hector did and they have now paid the price with their lives."

"Apology accepted," Allen said.

"Yeah, now let's get the fuck outta here," Clayton whispered to his father as the three men stood in unison, not speaking another word until they were out the building.

"What type of shit was that?" Kasir mumbled.

"I told you that old man was fuckin' crazy,"

Clayton said shaking his head as they got into their waiting SUV.

"I think we all knew he was crazy just not that crazy. Alejo know he could've slit them boys' throats after we left," Allen huffed. "He just wanted us to see the fuckin' blood too and ruin our afternoon," he added before chuckling.

"I think it was more than just that," Clayton replied, looking out the tinted window as the driver pulled out the parking lot.

"Then what?" Kasir questioned.

"I think old man Alejo was trying to make a point, not only to his family members but to us too."

"You might be right, Clayton."

"I know I'm right. We need to keep all eyes on Alejo 'cause I don't trust him. He might've killed his crooked ass nephews to show good faith but trust me that man hates to ever be wrong about anything. What he did to his nephews is probably what he really wanted to do to us but he knew nobody would've left that building alive. The only truth Alejo spoke in there was he was raised by wolves," Clayton scoffed leaning back in the car seat.

All three men remained silent for the duration of the drive. Each pondering what had transpired in what was supposed to be a simple business meeting that turned into a double homicide. They also thought about the point Clayton said Alejo was trying to make. No one wanted that to be true as their business with the Hernandez family was a lucrative one for everyone involved. But for men like Alejo, sometimes pride held more value than the almighty dollar, which made him extremely dangerous.

Coming soon

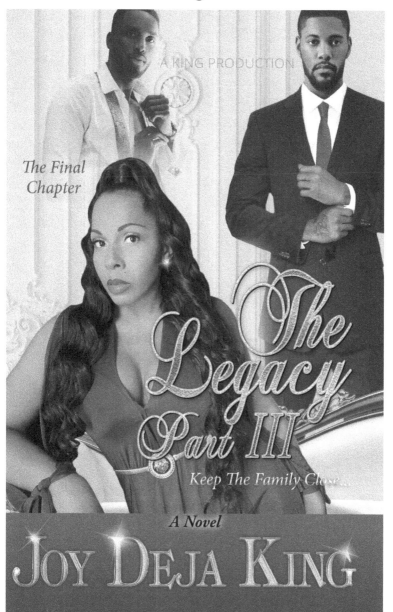

A KING PRODUCTION

# Sugar Babies...

**Toxic Series**

*A Titillating Tale*

*A Novelette*

# JOY DEJA KING

# Chapter One

## This Can't Be My Life

"You ungrateful bitch!" He spit in her face while gripping her neck as her legs dangled off the floor. His tone was sinister, and he had demons dancing in his eyes. "You thought I was going to let you leave me. It took time and knocking on a lot of doors, but I finally found you. I warned you not to fuck me over," he asserted before hurling her body against the wall.

"You're so sick," she uttered catching her breath. "I didn't fuck you over, you fucked yourself. I can't believe I ever thought I loved you," she cried as this predator slowly marched towards her. Fearing for her life, she grabbed the only thing within her reach to use as a potential weapon.

She swung the opalescent shimmer and smoke like swirl colored glass abstract sculpture, grazing the side of his head. The heavy figurine didn't make enough contact to do the damage she hoped but it did break the skin, causing a deep gash. The blood gushing from the laceration dripped into his eyes, making him disoriented long enough for her to use the opportunity to get away.

"I'ma kill you, you stupid bitch!" He roared as she sprinted across the room but before she reached the door the sound of gunshots brought everything to a halt.


### Six Months Earlier...


"Where the fuck am I?" Paige mumbled, pulling the silk sheet over her face to keep the glaring sun peeking through the large bedroom window out of her eyes. Her head was throbbing, and the symptoms of a hangover was in full effect the morning after a night of heavy drinking. Paige should've been over waking up to sensitivity to light and sound, nausea, stomach pain, dizziness, pounding headache, dry mouth and excessive thirst but instead she continued her hard partying ways.

"So sorry! I didn't realize anyone was here," the cleaning lady exclaimed when she noticed a svelte body shifting under the sheets.

"What time is it?" Paige questioned in an almost inaudible voice.

"Excuse me?"

Paige flung the sheet from over her face, "What time is it?"

"One o'clock, Miss. I'll let you sleep," the cleaning lady said turning to walk out the bedroom door.

"Wait!" Paige called out. She let out a deep sigh and rubbed her eyes, as her mind became more lucid. She rose in bed, focusing on the woman standing in the entryway with a cleaning bag strapped around her shoulder and waist. "Rosita!" she said with enthusiasm, happy her memory was back.

"Good day, Miss Paige," Rosita smiled.

"Please be a doll and bring me a strong cup of coffee."

"Will do."

"Wait!" Paige called out, once again stopping Rosita. "Where's Fitz?"

"Mr. Fitz not here. He not here when I arrive."

"Okay, thanks," Paige said reaching over to retrieve her phone off the nightstand. "Fuck," she huffed seeing all the missed calls from her father. She then read the text message from Fitz.

***Had to catch a flight to NY. Be back in a couple days. Call me when you wake up***

Right when Paige was about to call Fitz, her father was calling again. "Hello."

"Why haven't you called me back, Paige?" her father asked in a stern voice.

"Good morning to you too, daddy," she exhaled, praying and making false promises to herself that she would never get drunk again if her head would stop thumping.

"Don't you mean good afternoon," he countered.

"Of course, so what's up?"

"What are you doing?"

"Getting ready to head to class," she said

mouthing *thank you* to Rosita after she handed her a cup of coffee. Paige was desperate for a boost of caffeine.

"Really? I find that interesting since you got a letter from the dean today."

"Letter, did you read it?"

"This is my house, of course I read it."

"What did it say?" Paige pretended to want to know although her preference was to end the phone call.

"You received an academic dismissal because of your poor grades. You were given an opportunity to appeal to the committee members, but instead you chose to voluntarily drop out," her father stated. "I want an explanation. What is going on with you?"

*Fuck! I can't believe they sent that letter to my parent's house. I could've sworn I put the address to the condo down as the return address. This is some straight bullshit! Think! Think!* Paige screamed to herself.

"Paige, did you hear me?"

"Yes, I heard you," she said taking a few sips of coffee, hoping it would magically give her brain some power to quickly come up with a plausible lie.

"Then answer the question. Why did you

drop out of school and when did you plan on telling us...or was that not part of your plan?" he demanded to know.

"Daddy, would you please calm down," Paige said sweetly.

"No, I will not calm down. You told me you were on your way to class, which was obviously a lie. You flunked out of school. Probably due to you following behind that idiotic youtuber boy!" He shouted.

"Daddy, I told you he is a music artist that so happens to have a YouTube channel...with millions of followers mind you," she shot back defensively.

"Since you're no longer in school, are you planning on getting a job to support yourself?"

"Excuse me?" she stuttered. Shocked by the question, Paige placed her cup on the nightstand before she spilled it all over herself.

"How are you going to support yourself, Paige? Do you plan on getting a job?"

"I guess, but when you say support do you mean groceries and stuff?"

"Groceries, rent, car note, car insurance..."

"Daddy, I just turned twenty. I seriously doubt I can find a job that will pay all my bills," she scoffed.

"When you got your condo and I bought you a new car, it was with the understanding you would be attending college."

"I might go back to school. Like a reverse gap year. Instead of taking a year off right after I graduated from high school, I'm taking it now," she reasoned.

"Fine Paige, but you'll be taking that so called gap year from here."

"What do you mean here...I have to move back to Maryland?"

"That's exactly what I mean. I will not continue to pay your bills in Los Angeles when you're not in school full time. You can figure out what you want to do with your life from your home here in Maryland with your mother and I."

"You can't be serious! That isn't fair. I have a life here, friends. I can't just up and leave and move back to Maryland. Please daddy. Just give me six months to find myself. If I don't go back to school, then I'll get a job. I promise. But until I decide, you can't cut me off financially. It wouldn't be fair."

Paige could tell her pleas had the intended effect on her father and he was contemplating what she said. He inhaled and exhaled deeply before speaking. "Well, I suppose..."

"Let me speak to her!" Paige could hear her mother say to her father while grabbing his phone. "Paige Elizabeth Langston." She knew when her mother said her full name the conversation wouldn't end well.

"Yes mother."

"Your father will not be giving you another dime except to buy you a plane ticket to Maryland, so stop asking him. Do you understand me?"

"Gail, give me back the phone. I need to finish my conversation with our daughter," her father said but her mother was not having it.

"No. The only conversation you're having is with me. Paige, you can start packing your belongings. I'll be in touch with your flight details," her mother said and ended the call.

Paige let out a high-pitched scream and threw her iPhone across the room. "This can't be my life!"

A KING PRODUCTION

# Stackin' PAPER

*a novel*

# JOY DEJA KING

# *Chapter One*

## A Killer Is Born

**Philly, 1993**

"Please, Daquan, don't hit me again!" the young mother screamed, covering her face in defense mode. She hurriedly pushed herself away from her predator, sliding her body on the cold hardwood floor.

"Bitch, get yo' ass back over here!" he barked, grabbing her matted black hair and dragging her into the kitchen. He reached for the hot skillet from the top of the oven, and you could hear the oil popping underneath the fried chicken his wife had been cooking right before he came home.

"Didn't I tell you to have my food ready on the table when I came home?"

"I... I... I was almost finished, but you came home early," Teresa stuttered, "Ouch!" she yelled as her neck damn near snapped when Daquan gripped her hair even tighter.

"I don't want to hear your fuckin' excuses. That's what yo' problem is. You so damn hard headed and neva want to listen. But like they say, a hard head make fo' a soft ass. You gon' learn to listen to me."

"Please, please, Daquan, don't do this! Let me finish frying your chicken and I'll never do this again. Your food will be ready and on the table everyday on time. I promise!"

"I'm tired of hearing your damn excuses."

*"Bang!"* was all you heard as the hot skillet came crashing down on Teresa's head. The hot oil splashed up in the air, and if Daquan hadn't moved forward and turned his head, his face would've been saturated with the grease.

But Teresa wasn't so lucky, as the burning oil grazed her hands, as they were protecting her face and part of her thigh.

After belting out in pain from the grease, she then noticed blood trickling down from the open gash on the side of her forehead. But it didn't stop there. Daquan then put the skillet down and began kicking Teresa in her ribs and back like she was a diseased infected dog that had just bitten him.

"Yo', Pops, leave moms alone! Why you always got to do this? It ain't never no peace when you come in this house." Genesis stood in the kitchen entrance with his fists clenched and panting like a bull. He had grown sick and tired of watching his father beat his mother down almost every single day. At the age of eleven he had seen his mother receive more ass whippings than hugs or any indication of love.

"Boy, who the fuck you talkin' to? You betta get yo' ass back in your room and stay the hell outta of grown people's business." "Genesis, listen to your father. I'll be alright. Now go back to your room," his mother pleaded.

Genesis just stood there unable to move, watching his mother and feeling helpless. The blood was now covering her white nightgown and she was covering her midsection, obviously in pain trying to protect the baby that was growing inside of her. He was in a trance, not knowing what to do to make the madness stop. But he was quickly brought back to reality when he felt his jaw almost crack from the punch his father landed on the side of his face.

"I ain't gon' tell you again. Get yo' ass back in your room! And don't come out until I tell you to! Now go!" Daquan didn't even wait to let his only son go back to his room. He immediately went over to Teresa and picked up where he left off, punishing her body with punches and kicks. He seemed oblivious to the fact that not only was he killing her, but also he was killing his unborn child right before his son's eyes.

A tear streamed down Genesis's face as he tried to reflect on one happy time he had with his dad, but he went blank. There were no happy times. From the first moment he could remember, his dad was a monster.

All Genesis remembered starting from the age of three was the constant beat downs his mother endured for no reason. If his dad's clothes weren't ironed just right, then a blow to the face. If the volume of the television was too loud, then a jab here. And, God forbid, if the small, two-bedroom apartment in the drug-infested building they lived in wasn't spotless, a nuclear bomb would explode in the form of Daquan. But the crazy part was, no matter how clean their apartment was or how good the food was cooked and his clothes being ironed just right, it was never good enough. Daquan would bust in the door, drunk or high, full of anger, ready to take out all his frustration out on his wife. The dead end jobs, being broke, living in the drug infested and violent prone city of Philadelphia had turned the already troubled man into poison to his whole family.

"Daddy, leave my mom alone," Genesis said in a calm, unemotional tone. Daquan kept striking Teresa as if he didn't hear his son. "I'm not gonna to tell you again. Leave my mom alone." This time Daquan heard his son's warning but seemed unfazed.

"I guess that swollen jaw wasn't enough for you. You dying to get that ass beat." Daquan looked down at a now black and blue Teresa who seemed to be about to take her last breath. "You keep yo' ass right here, while I teach our son a lesson." Teresa reached her hand out with the little strength she had left trying to save her son. But she quickly realized it was too late. The sins of the parents had now falling upon their child.

"Get away from my mother. I want you to leave and don't ever come back."

Daquan was so caught up in the lashing he had been putting on his wife that he didn't even notice Genesis retrieving the gun he left on the kitchen counter until he had it raised and pointed in his direction. "Lil' fuck, you un lost yo' damn mind! You gon' make me beat you with the tip of my gun."

Daquan reached his hand out to grab the gun out of Genesis's hand, and when he moved his leg forward, it would be the last step he'd ever take in his life. The single shot fired ripped through Daquan's heart and he collapsed on the kitchen floor, dying instantly.

Genesis was frozen and his mother began crying hysterically.

"Oh dear God!" Teresa moaned, trying to gasp for air. "Oh, Genesis baby, what have you done?" She stared at Daquan, who laid face up with his eyes wide open in shock. He died not believing until it was too late that his own son would be the one to take him out this world.

It wasn't until they heard the pounding on the front door that Genesis snapped back to the severity of the situation at hand.

"Is everything alright in there?" they heard the older lady from across the hall ask.

Genesis walked to the door still gripping the .380-caliber semi-automatic. He opened the door and said in a serene voice, "No, Ms. Johnson, everything is *not* alright. I just killed my father."

****

Two months later, Teresa cried as she watched her son being taking away to spend a minimum of two years in a juvenile facility in Pemberton, New Jersey.

Although it was obvious by the bruises on both Teresa and Genesis that he acted in self defense, the judge felt that the young boy having to live with the guilt of murdering his own father wasn't punishment enough. He concluded that if Genesis didn't get a hard wake up call, he would be headed on a path of self destruction. He first ordered him to stay at the juvenile facility until he was eighteen. But after pleas from his mother, neighbors and his teacher, who testified that Genesis had the ability to accomplish whatever he wanted in life because of how smart and gifted he was, the judge reduced it to two years, but only if he demonstrated excellent behavior during his time there. Those two years turned into four and four turned into seven. At the age of eighteen when Genesis was finally released he was no longer a young boy, he was now a criminal minded man.

# Read The Entire Bitch Series in This Order

## ORDER FORM

**Name:**

**Address:**

**City/State:**

**Zip:**

| QUANTITY | TITLES | PRICE | TOTAL |
|---|---|---|---|
| | Bitch | $15.00 | |
| | Bitch Reloaded | $15.00 | |
| | The Bitch Is Back | $15.00 | |
| | Queen Bitch | $15.00 | |
| | Last Bitch Standing | $15.00 | |
| | Superstar | $15.00 | |
| | Ride Wit' Me | $12.00 | |
| | Ride Wit' Me Part 2 | $15.00 | |
| | Stackin' Paper | $15.00 | |
| | Trife Life To Lavish | $15.00 | |
| | Trife Life To Lavish II | $15.00 | |
| | Stackin' Paper II | $15.00 | |
| | Rich or Famous | $15.00 | |
| | Rich or Famous Part 2 | $15.00 | |
| | Rich or Famous Part 3 | $15.00 | |
| | Bitch A New Beginning | $15.00 | |
| | Mafia Princess Part 1 | $15.00 | |
| | Mafia Princess Part 2 | $15.00 | |
| | Mafia Princess Part 3 | $15.00 | |
| | Mafia Princess Part 4 | $15.00 | |
| | Mafia Princess Part 5 | $15.00 | |
| | Boss Bitch | $15.00 | |
| | Baller Bitches Vol. 1 | $15.00 | |
| | Baller Bitches Vol. 2 | $15.00 | |
| | Baller Bitches Vol. 3 | $15.00 | |
| | Bad Bitch | $15.00 | |
| | Still The Baddest Bitch | $15.00 | |
| | Power | $15.00 | |
| | Power Part 2 | $15.00 | |
| | Drake | $15.00 | |
| | Drake Part 2 | $15.00 | |
| | Female Hustler | $15.00 | |
| | Female Hustler Part 2 | $15.00 | |
| | Female Hustler Part 3 | $15.00 | |
| | Female Hustler Part 4 | $15.00 | |
| | Female Hustler Part 5 | $15.00 | |
| | Female Hustler Part 6 | $15.00 | |
| | Princess Fever "Birthday Bash" | $6.00 | |
| | Nico Carter The Men Of The Bitch Series | $15.00 | |
| | Bitch The Beginning Of The End | $15.00 | |
| | Supreme...Men Of The Bitch Series | $15.00 | |
| | Bitch The Final Chapter | $15.00 | |
| | Stackin' Paper III | $15.00 | |
| | Men Of The Bitch Series And The Women Who Love Them | $15.00 | |
| | Coke Like The 80s | $15.00 | |
| | Baller Bitches The Reunion Vol. 4 | $15.00 | |
| | Stackin' Paper IV | $15.00 | |
| | The Legacy | $15.00 | |
| | Lovin' Thy Enemy | $15.00 | |
| | Stackin' Paper V | $15.00 | |
| | The Legacy Part 2 | $15.00 | |
| | Assassins - Episode 1 | $11.00 | |
| | Assassins - Episode 2 | $11.00 | |
| | Assassins - Episode 2 | $11.00 | |
| | Bitch Chronicles | $40.00 | |
| | So Hood So Rich | $15.00 | |
| | Stackin' Paper VI | $15.00 | |
| | Female Hustler Part 7 | $15.00 | |
| | Toxic... | $6.00 | |
| | Stackin' Paper VII | $15.00 | |
| | Sugar Babies... | $9.99 | |
| | Deadly Divorce... | $11.99 | |

**Shipping/Handling (Via Priority Mail)** $8.95 1-3 Books, $16.25 4-7 Books. For 7 or more $21.50. Total: $_____ FORMS OF
**ACCEPTED PAYMENTS:** Certified or government issued checks and money Orders, all mail in orders take 5-7 Business days to be delivered

CPSIA information can be obtained
at www.ICGtesting.com
Printed in the USA
LVHW042350170822
726201LV00001B/137